THE
TOWN
MOUSE
AND THE
COUNTRY
MOUSE

For the mouse that knows
his own mind – Helen

A TEMPLAR BOOK

First published in the UK in 2011 by Templar Publishing
This softback edition published in 2012 by Templar Publishing,
an imprint of The Templar Company Limited,
The Granary, North Street, Dorking, Surrey, RH4 1DN, UK
www.templarco.co.uk

Copyright © 2011 by Helen Ward

First softback edition

ISBN 978-1-84877-492-6

Edited by A. J. Wood

Printed in China

THE TOWN MOUSE AND THE COUNTRY MOUSE

AN AESOP FABLE
RETOLD &
ILLUSTRATED BY

HELEN WARD

templar publishing
www.templarco.co.uk

There was once
merely a mouse.

He lived a small
and quiet life
among the seasons.

He knew the
busyness of Summer
and the rich, ripe,
dozy-sweet days
of Autumn.

He knew the aching hunger
of a long, cold Winter
under the snow,
and the smell of the
warming earth in the first
days of Spring.

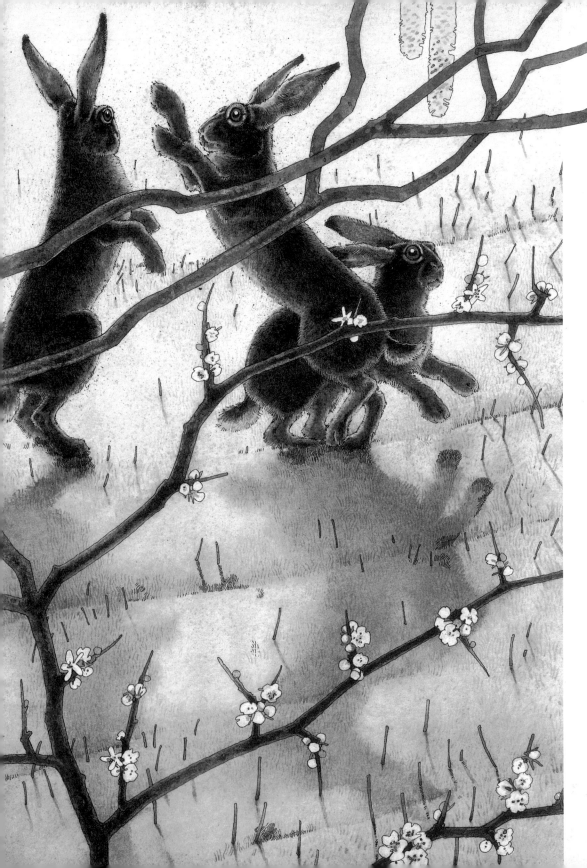

The Country Mouse knew
he was contented.

Then, one Spring morning
a visitor arrived…
a fine, sleek City cousin
with a lot to say.

"In the city,
we don't have mud…

and we don't have
dangerous wild animals.

"In our city, we dine
on rich, exotic foods in
sumptuous surroundings.

"We have such amazing
sights and sounds.
We have noise and
bustle and hum.
You should visit.
You should come and
see the wonders of
my electric city."

Left to his own thoughts
the Country Mouse
grew less certain
of his contentedness.

He felt a longing for
new sights and sounds.

With the first sharp chill
of Winter he stole a ride
to that bustle and hum.

The electric city crowded
his ears and eyes.

He gazed at the high
horizon where the cold sky
was propped up on
great towers of smooth
stone and glass.

He found lights
in the dark…

and automatic
ups and downs.

He found his cousin's
well-appointed apartment,
with luxurious
accommodation for
the humblest of
creatures.

But, settling to sleep
among glorious
treasures and refined,
tissuey bedding,
the guest room became
suddenly unstable…

As he hid,
he recalled the homely
certainties of his own
grassy
nest.

Eventually his grumbling
stomach and sharp nose
drew him to a table.
It was just as glamorous
as the tales his cousin
had told.

A magnificent feast,
so delicious, so sweet,
so perfect...

But so perilous.

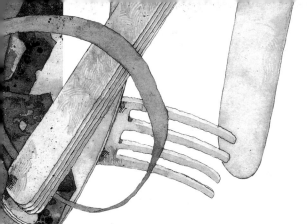

As he ran,
he remembered
with fondness his own
quiet meals and their
more modest variety.

He remembered too
the song of the
faraway thrush,
the heave of the worm
in the close earth,
and the buzz of crickets
in the hot hay meadows.

He longed
to be elsewhere.
To see the night sky
lit only by stars.

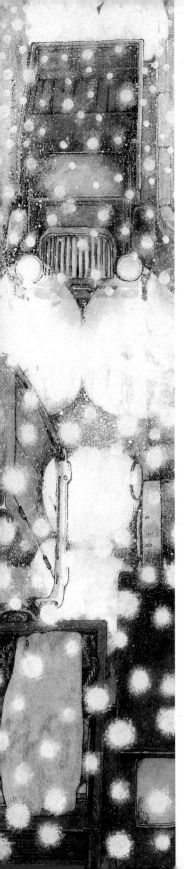

To be safe,
to be contented,
to be home.

And once he was home…

He slept deeply.

Merely a mouse
dreaming of Spring.

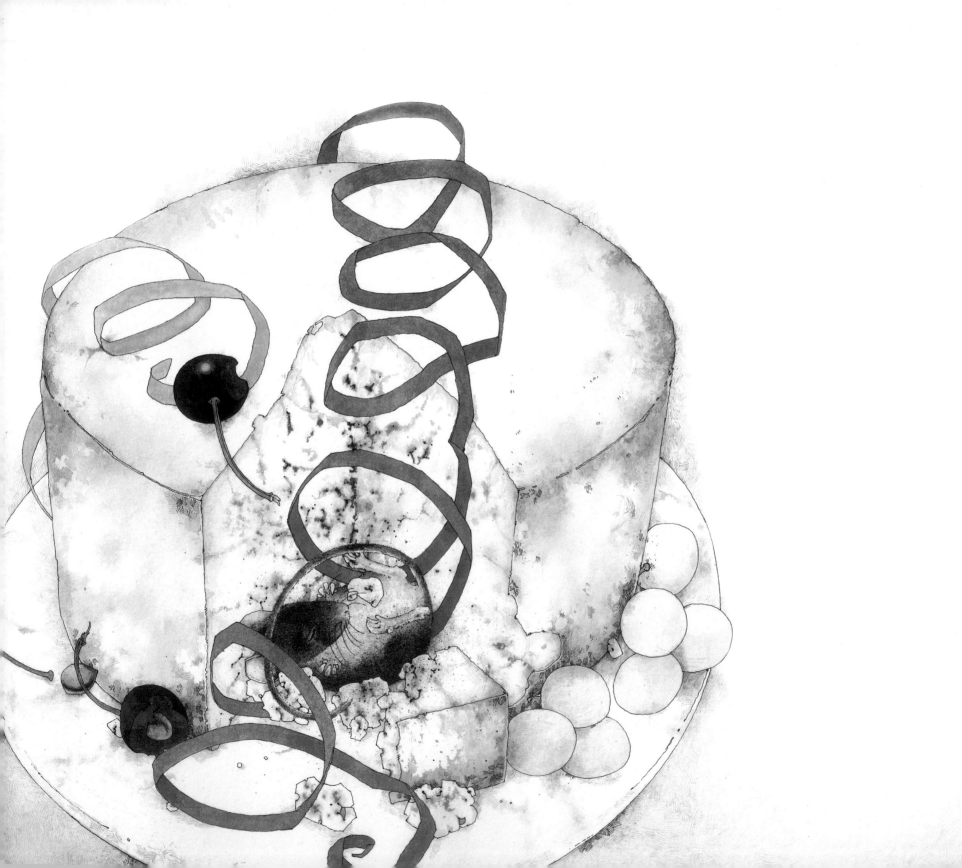